World of Reading

LEVEL 1

THE MIGHTY THOR

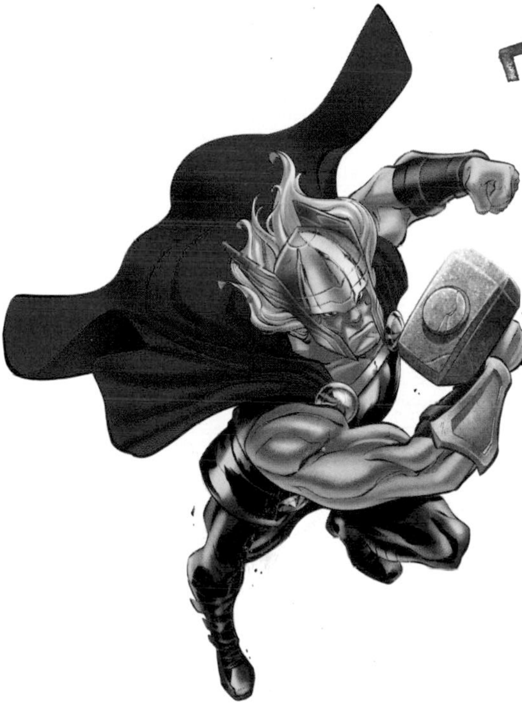

THIS IS THOR

Written by Alexandra West

Illustrated by Roberto Di Salvo, Simone Boufantino, and Tomasso Moscardini

Based on the Marvel comic book series *Thor*

MARVEL

Los Angeles
New York

MARVEL

marvelkids.com

© 2017 MARVEL

SUSTAINABLE FORESTRY INITIATIVE

Certified Chain of Custody
At Least 20% Certified Forest Content
www.sfiprogram.org
SFI-00993

ISBN 978-1-368-01128-0
FAC-029261-17230
Printed in the United States of America
First Edition, October 2017
1 3 5 7 9 10 8 6 4 2

This is Thor.

Thor lives on Asgard.
It is a planet in space.

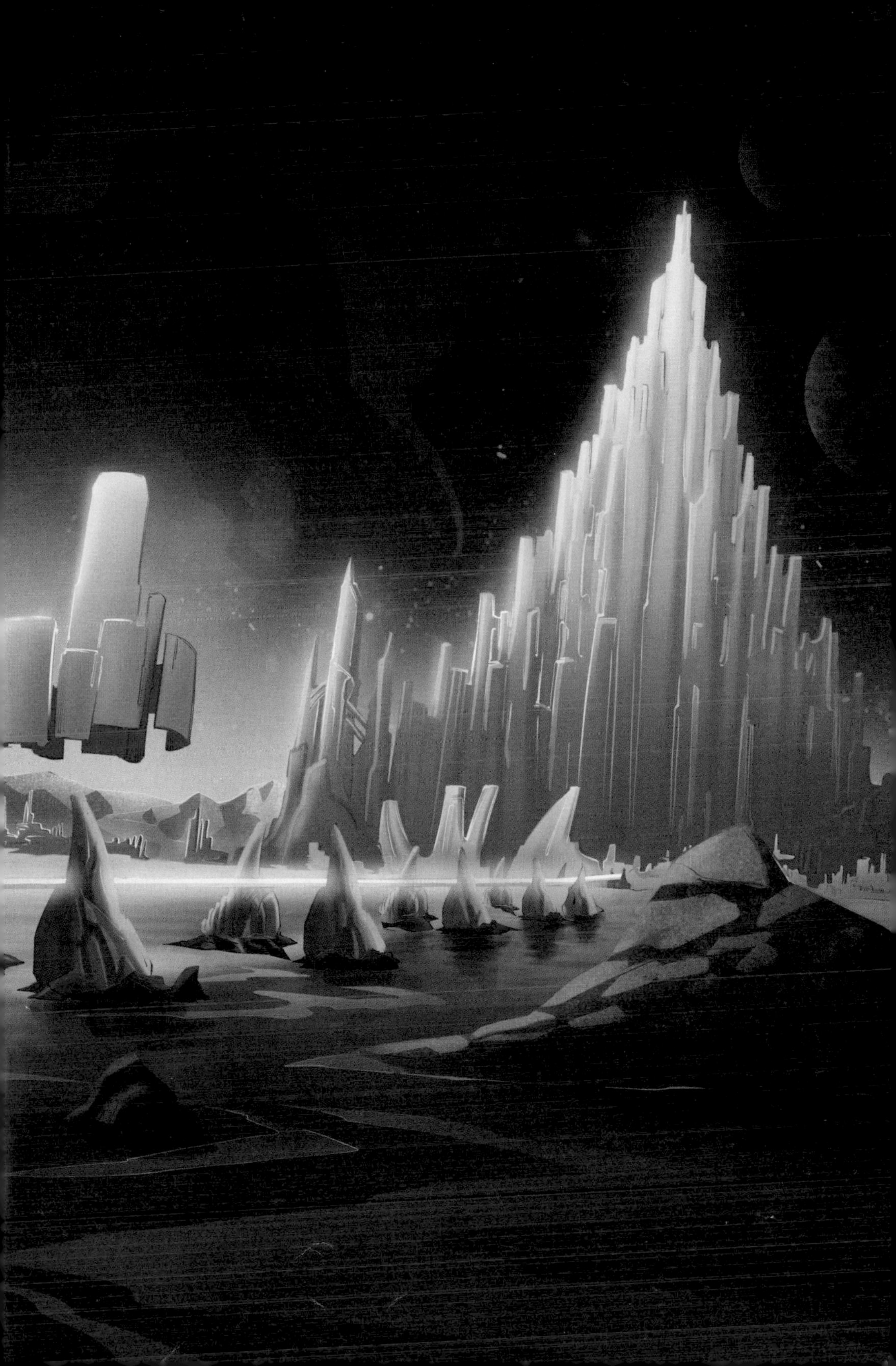

Thor and Loki are
the sons of King Odin.
They grow up together.

King Odin makes a
magic hammer.
The hammer is for Thor.

Thor is the favorite son.
Loki is jealous of Thor.

The hammer is heavy.
Thor cannot lift the hammer.
Only a person who is
worthy can lift it.

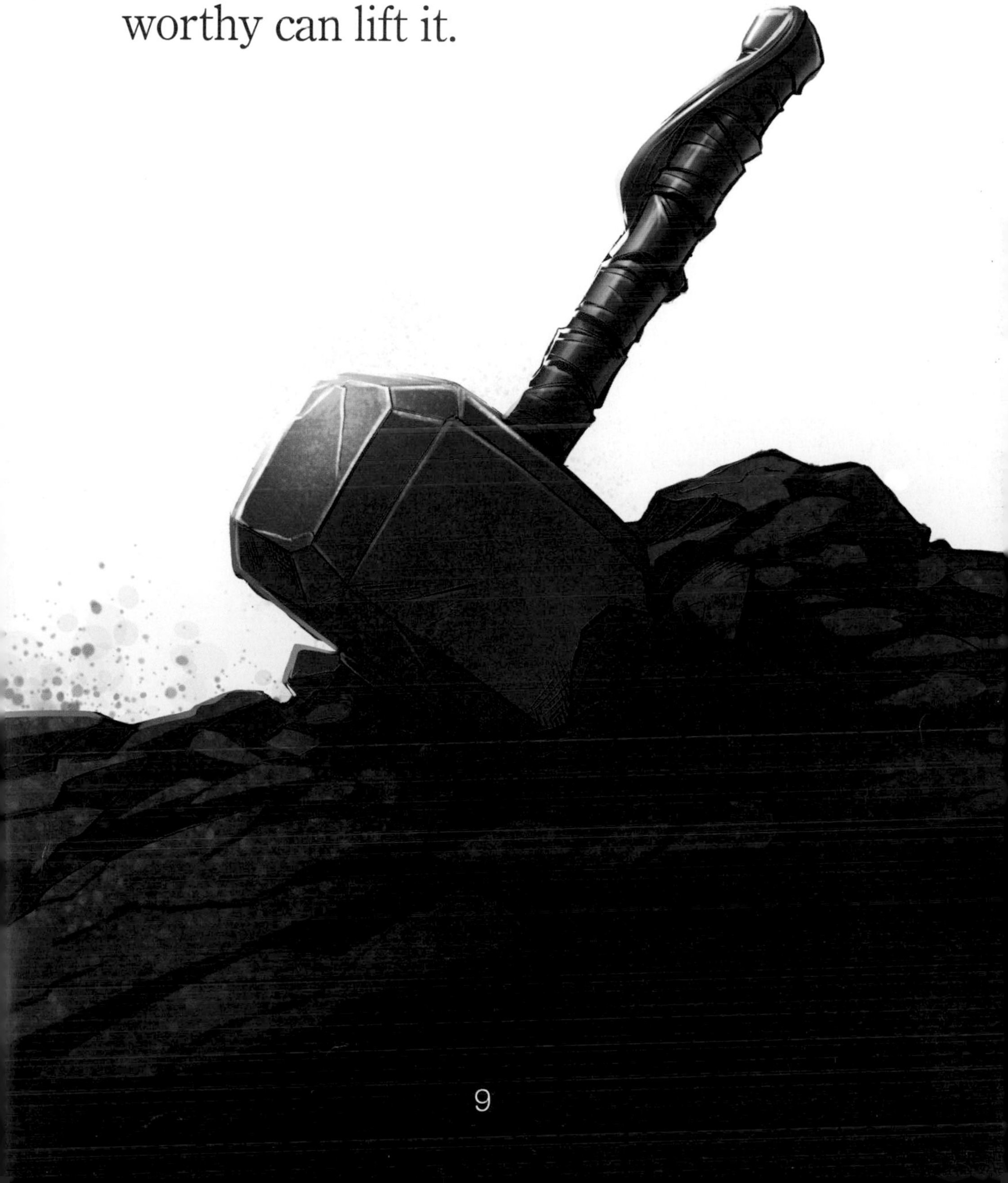

Thor works hard
to be worthy.

Thor fights great beasts.
He shows he can be brave.

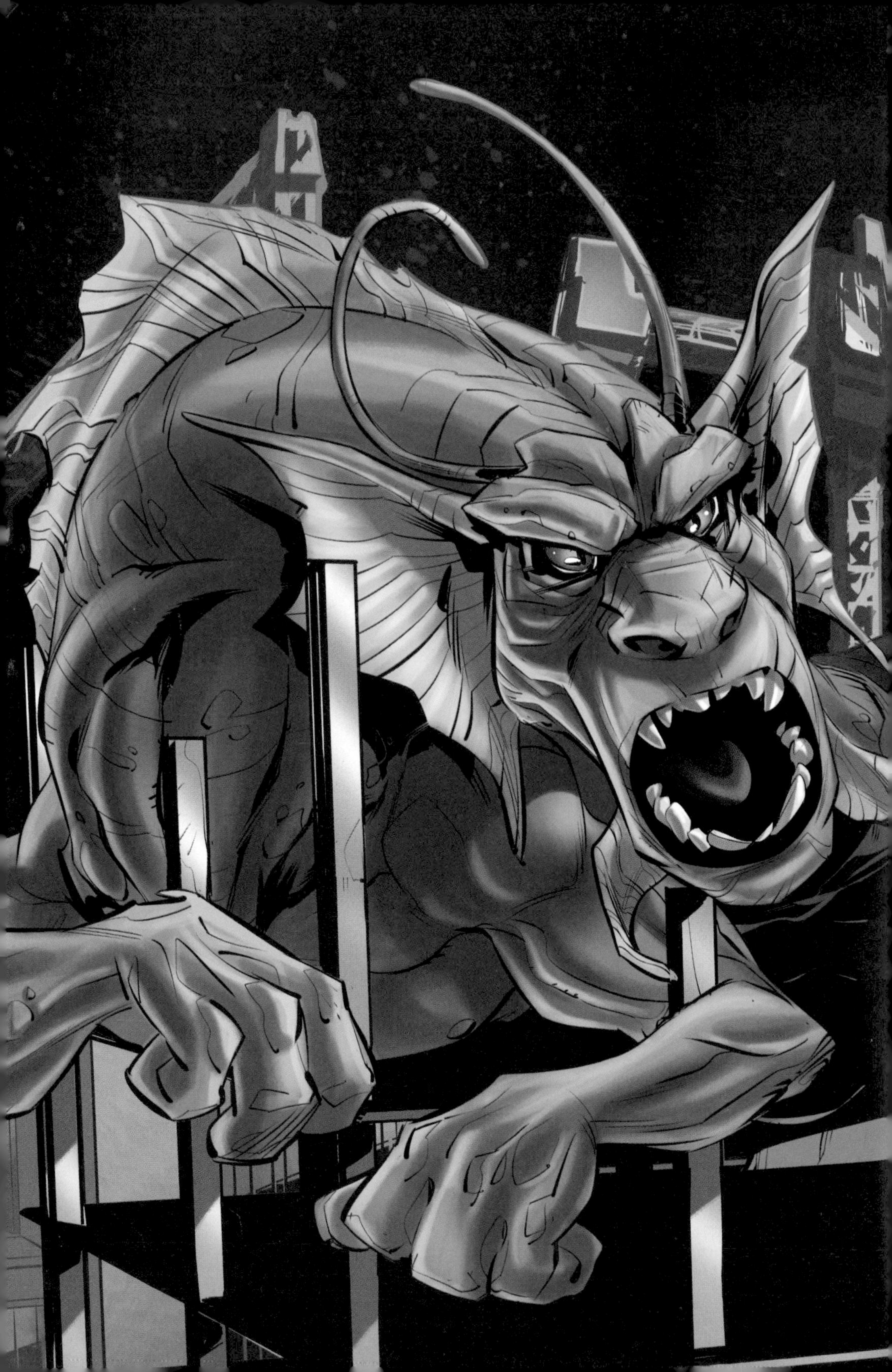

Thor fights big monsters.
He shows he can be strong.

Thor tries again.
He lifts the hammer.
Thor is finally worthy!

Thor throws his hammer.
It flies back to him.

Thor stamps his hammer
on the ground.

Thor twirls his hammer
to fly through the sky.

Thor shows off his power.
He is very selfish.

King Odin sees Thor.
He is very angry.

King Odin curses
Thor to live on Earth.

Thor must be a human.
His name is Don Blake.
He is a doctor.

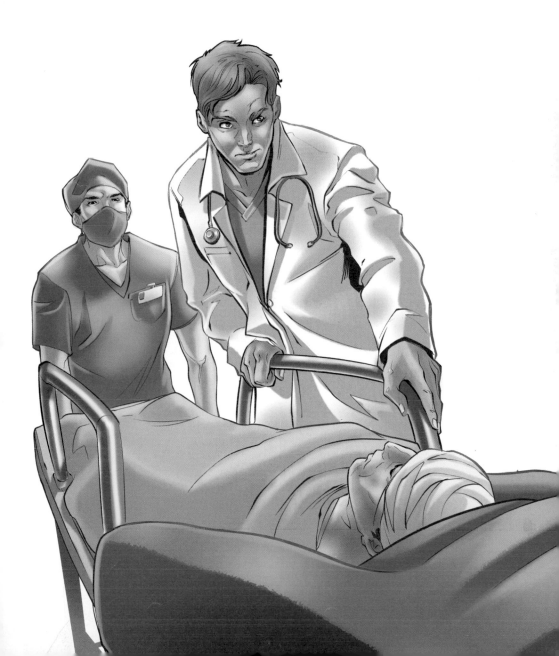

Don Blake helps people.
He finds his hammer.
Don Blake becomes Thor!
The curse is broken.

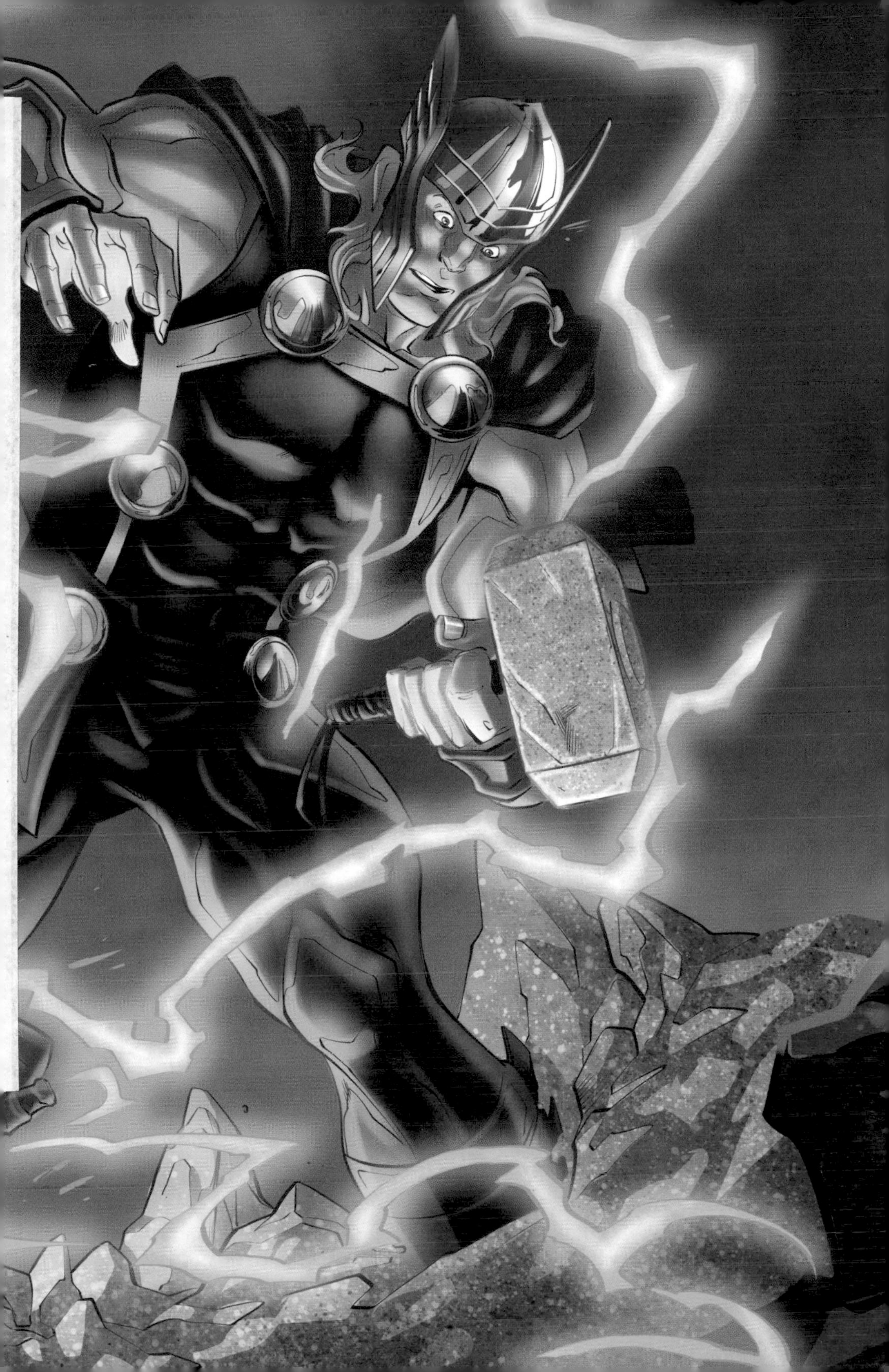

Thor has his powers back.
He is the Mighty Thor.

Loki learns dark magic.
He is evil.
He sees Thor on Earth.
Loki has an idea.

Loki makes Hulk angry.
Hulk attacks Thor.

Thor fights back!
He realizes Loki
tricked Hulk.

Thor decides to be
a force for good.
He will defeat evil.

Thor has an idea.
He flies away.

Thor cannot defeat
evil alone.
He joins a team.
He joins the Avengers!

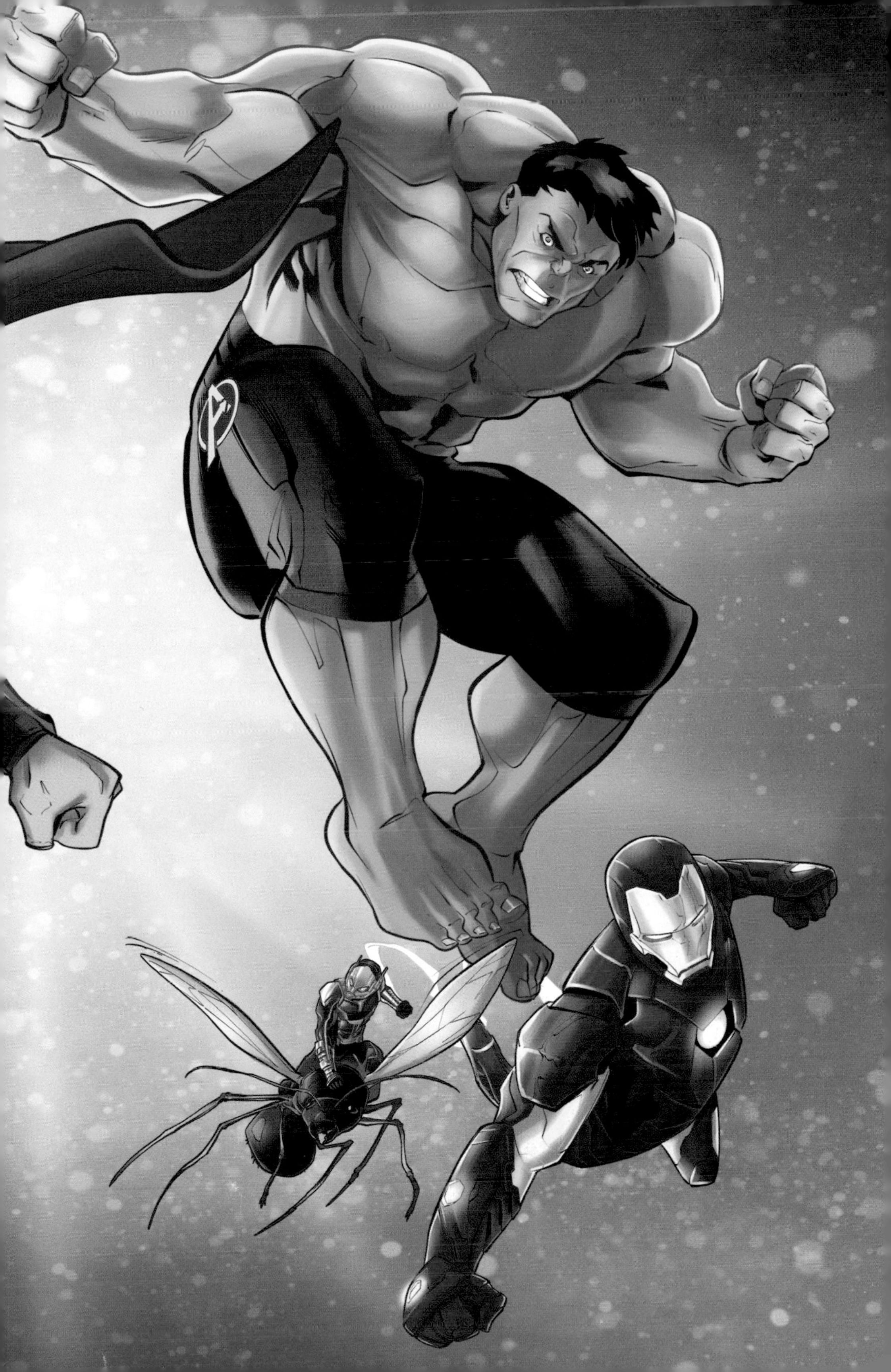

Thor is the Mighty Avenger.